How many times can you find **ELSA** in the puzzle?
Look up, down, forward, and backward.

E	A	S	L	E	E
A	S	A	S	L	E
E	L	S	A	S	E
S	E	L	S	A	L

ANSWER: 6.

Circle the snowflakes that have the letters in Anna's name.

Solve the maze to help Anna find her big sister, Elsa.

START

FINISH

ANSWER:

Anna and Elsa love to play together!

Circle all the pictures of Elsa.
How many pictures of Anna are left?

Elsa has a secret! Use the key to find out what it is.

Elsa uses her magical ice powers to create
a winter wonderland inside the castle!

Anna and Elsa build a snowman!

Draw some friends for this snowman.

Count the snowmen on this page. How many are there?

One of Elsa's magic ice blasts hits Anna by mistake.
It makes Anna very cold!

The king and queen rush the girls to the trolls.
They hope the trolls' magic can help them!

Look at the top picture carefully. Then circle five things that are different in the bottom picture.

Look up, down, forward, and backward to find the names of the royal family.

King Queen Anna Elsa

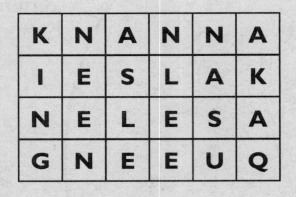

K	N	A	N	N	A
I	E	S	L	A	K
N	E	L	E	S	A
G	N	E	E	U	Q

The trolls help Anna, but Elsa is forced to wear gloves to keep everyone safe from her ice powers.

Color the picture of the king and Elsa that is different from the others.

Circle the two pictures of Elsa that are exactly the same.

After the accident, Elsa won't play with Anna.
She is afraid she might hurt her sister again.

Anna is lonely without her sister.

Many years later, a grown-up Elsa prepares
to become Queen of Arendelle.

Circle the shadow that matches the image
of Anna and Elsa on this page.

A

B

C

D

© Disney

Kristoff is an ice harvester. He is going to
Arendelle to sell ice at Elsa's coronation ceremony.

Anna is excited! Lots of people arrive
in Arendelle for the ceremony.

Elsa is scared. She tries to control her ice power, but without her gloves, she freezes everything she touches!

Color Elsa's royal outfit.

To find out the name of this naval officer, follow the lines and write each letter on the correct blank.

_ _ _ _ _ _ _ _   _ _ _ _ _

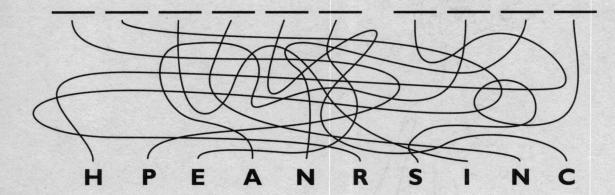

H P E A N R S I N C

Prince Hans has sailed to Arendelle from afar.

Complete the picture of Prince Hans.

How many ships are on this page?

Draw flags and sails on this boat.

Prince Hans meets Princess Anna.
He helps her when she stumbles.

Princess Anna returns to the castle—
but she can't stop thinking about Prince Hans.

Design a new dress for Anna.

How many times can you find CASTLE in the puzzle?
Look up, down, forward, and backward.

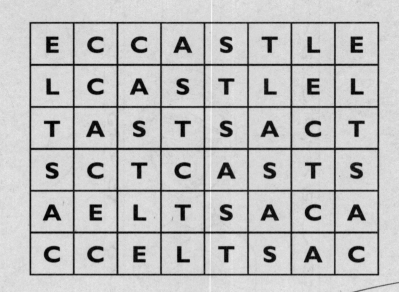

E	C	C	A	S	T	L	E
L	C	A	S	T	L	E	L
T	A	S	T	S	A	C	T
S	C	T	C	A	S	T	S
A	E	L	T	S	A	C	A
C	C	E	L	T	S	A	C

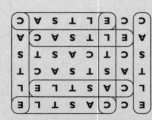

Draw a beautiful princess.

Design a special dress for Princess Elsa's coronation.

Elsa makes it through the ceremony with freezing anything!

Princess Elsa will be the new queen. Draw a crown for her.

Elsa is crowned Queen of Arendelle!

How many times can you find **CROWN** in the puzzle?
Look up, down, forward, backward, and diagonally.

N	W	C	R	O	W	N
W	O	R	O	W	N	W
C	R	O	W	N	W	O
R	N	W	R	O	N	R
C	R	N	W	O	R	C

Anna shares a dance with Prince Hans.

Look up, down, forward, and backward to find the words below.

princess prince castle crown royal kingdom

F	B	E	C	N	I	R	P
A	Y	K	U	E	O	P	R
E	V	I	W	G	H	J	I
L	Z	N	W	O	R	C	N
T	X	G	C	V	B	N	C
S	B	D	F	G	H	J	E
A	R	O	Y	A	L	F	S
C	R	M	O	N	K	B	S

Circle the two pictures of Anna and Prince Hans that are exactly the same.

1

2

3

4

ANSWER: 2 and 3.

Anna falls in love with Prince Hans.
He asks her to marry him, and she says yes!

Look at the top picture carefully.
Then circle four things that are different in the bottom picture.

ANSWER: There is no flower in Anna's hair; there are only two ribbons in her hair; the buttons are missing from Hans's jacket; and the design is missing from the collar.

Anna tells Elsa that she and Prince Hans are engaged.
Elsa thinks it's too soon.

Why is Anna upset with Elsa? To find out, start at the arrow and, going clockwise around the circle, write the letters in order on the blanks.

▼

ELSAWONTALLOWANNATOMARRYHANS

_ _ _ _ _ , _ _ _ '_

_ _ _ _ _ _ _ _ _ _ _

_ _ _ _ _ _ _ _ _ !

ANSWER: Elsa won't allow Anna to marry Hans!

What are they saying? Write it in their speech balloons.

After an argument with Anna,
Elsa loses control of her magical ice powers!

Everyone is shocked by Elsa's ice power!

Complete the snowflake.

After revealing her ice power, Elsa runs away from Arendelle!

Anna must go after her sister. She asks Prince Hans
to take care of the kingdom while she's away.

How many words can you make using the letters in
KINGDOM?

_____   _____

_____   _____

_____   _____

_____   _____

_____   _____

_____   _____

_____   _____

_____   _____

All alone in the mountains, Elsa is free to use her ice powers.

Elsa builds a magnificent ice palace on the North Mountain.

Fill this page with snowflakes!

What else does Elsa create? To find out, start at
the arrow and, going clockwise around the circle, write
every other letter in order on the blanks.

_ _ _ _   _ _ _ _ _ _

_   _ _ _ _ _ _ _ _ _

_ _ _ _ _ _ !

Elsa becomes the Snow Queen!

Anna follows her sister!

Solve the maze to help Anna get started!

START

FINISH

ANSWER:

Anna gets caught in a snowstorm!
Find the path that leads Anna to Oaken's store.

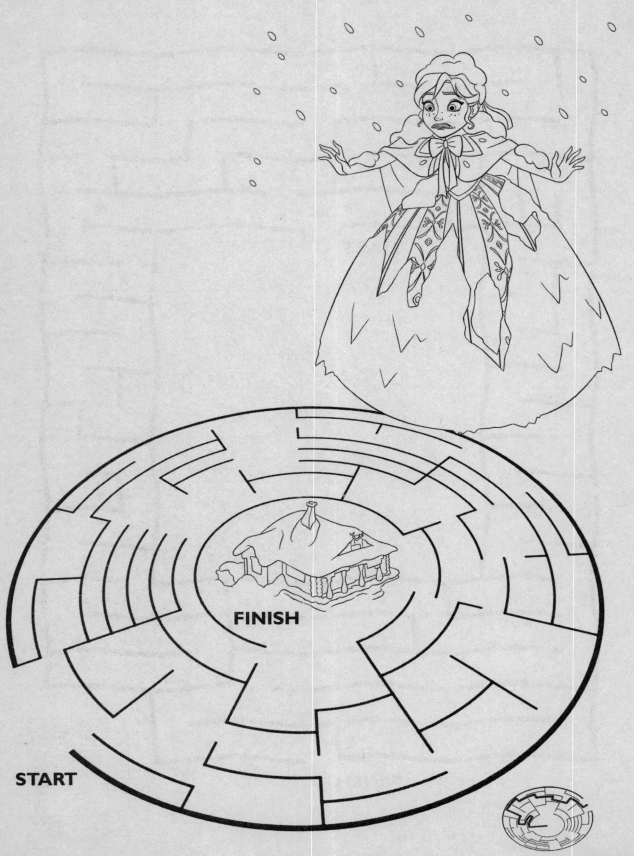

FINISH

START

How many words can you make using the letters in
WEATHER?

_____   _____

_____   _____

_____   _____

_____   _____

_____   _____

_____   _____

_____   _____

_____   _____

_____   _____

POSSIBLE ANSWERS: Are, at, ate, awe, ear, eat, era, earth, hat, hare, heart, heat, heater, her, here, rate, raw, tea, tear, tee, thaw, the, there, three, tree, war, water, wear, were, wet, what, and wheat.

Look up, down, forward, and backward to find the words below.
ice snow frozen storm cold cloud

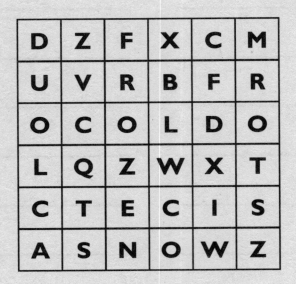

D	Z	F	X	C	M
U	V	R	B	F	R
O	C	O	L	D	O
L	Q	Z	W	X	T
C	T	E	C	I	S
A	S	N	O	W	Z

To find out the name of this big man,
follow the lines and write each letter on the correct blank.

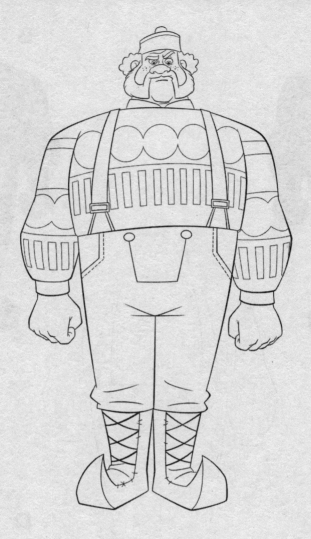

_ _ _ _ _

N K E A O

Circle Oaken's shadow.

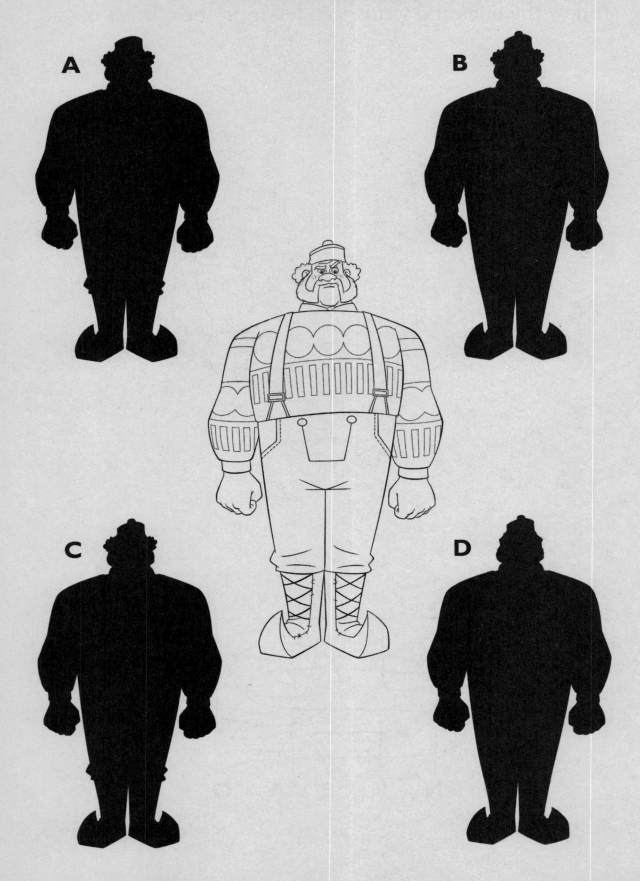

Oaken is a very large man—so don't make him mad!

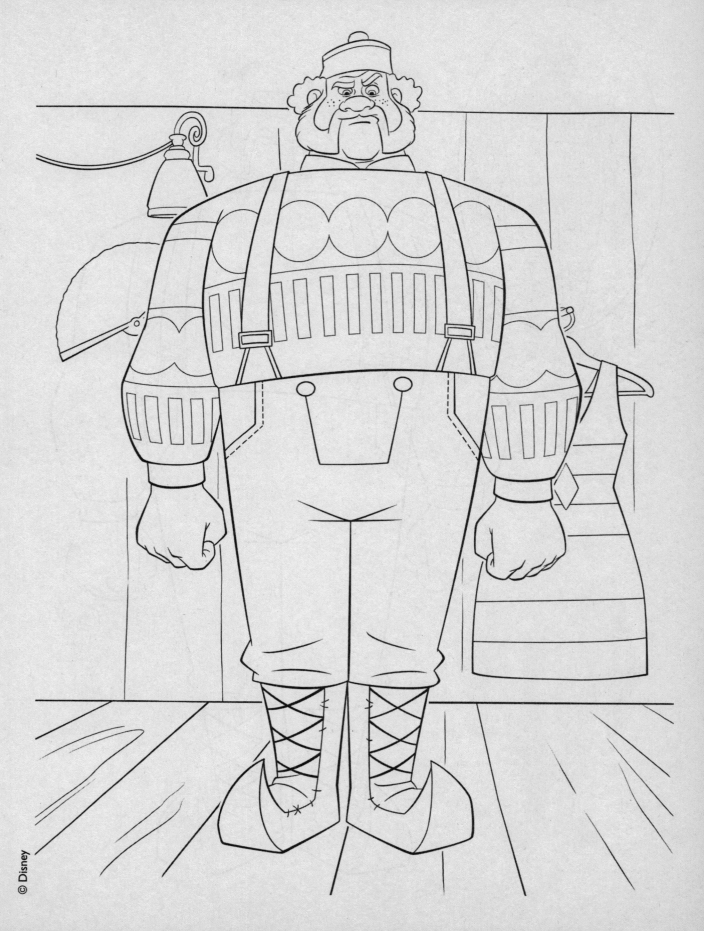

Complete the picture of Oaken.

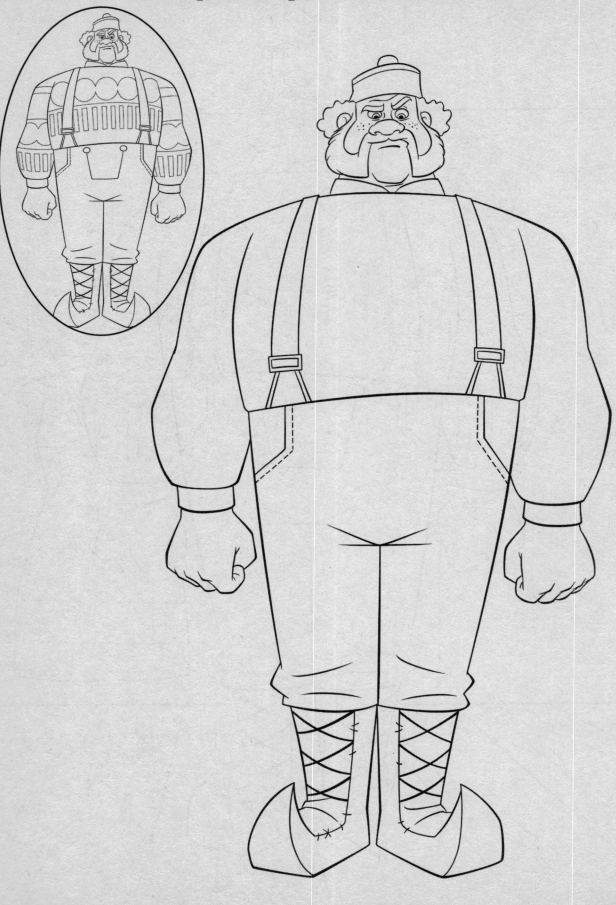

To find out the name of this mountain man,
follow the lines and write each letter on the correct blank.

_____.

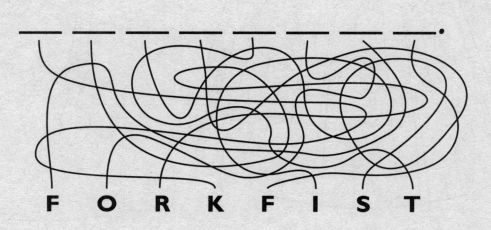

F O R K F I S T

Anna meets a snow-covered Kristoff.
Maybe he can help Anna find her sister!

How many times can you find **KRISTOFF** in the puzzle?
Look up, down, forward, and backward.

O	K	R	I	S	T	O	F	F	F
K	R	I	S	T	O	F	F	O	F
F	I	F	R	K	R	F	F	O	O
K	S	F	F	F	O	K	R	I	T
R	T	O	K	R	I	R	K	R	S
F	O	F	R	K	R	F	F	O	I
I	F	F	O	T	S	I	R	K	R
K	F	F	F	O	T	S	I	R	K

Kristoff calls Oaken a crook—and gets thrown out of the store!

Circle the shadow that belongs to Kristoff.

A

B

C

D

ANSWER: B.

Complete the picture of Kristoff.

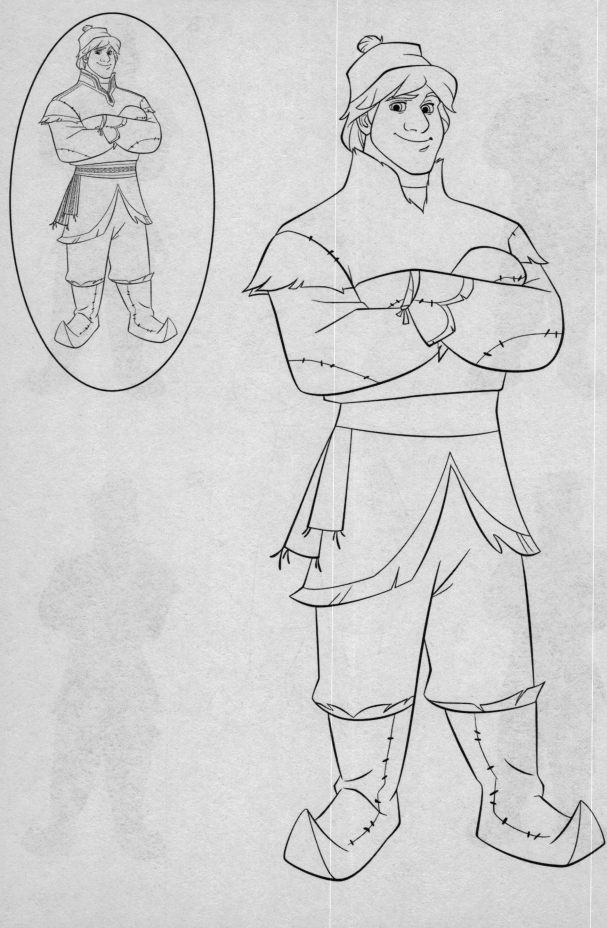

How many words can you make using the letters in
KRISTOFF?

_____   _____

_____   _____

_____   _____

_____   _____

_____   _____

_____   _____

_____   _____

_____   _____

POSSIBLE ANSWERS: First, fist, rift, fir, fit, stir, is, it, of, off, or, and rot.

To find out the name of this reindeer, circle every third letter.
Then write those letters in order on the blanks.

Z M S B G V X Y E F R N

— — — —

Solve the maze to help Kristoff find Sven.

START

FINISH

ANSWER:

Circle Sven's shadow.

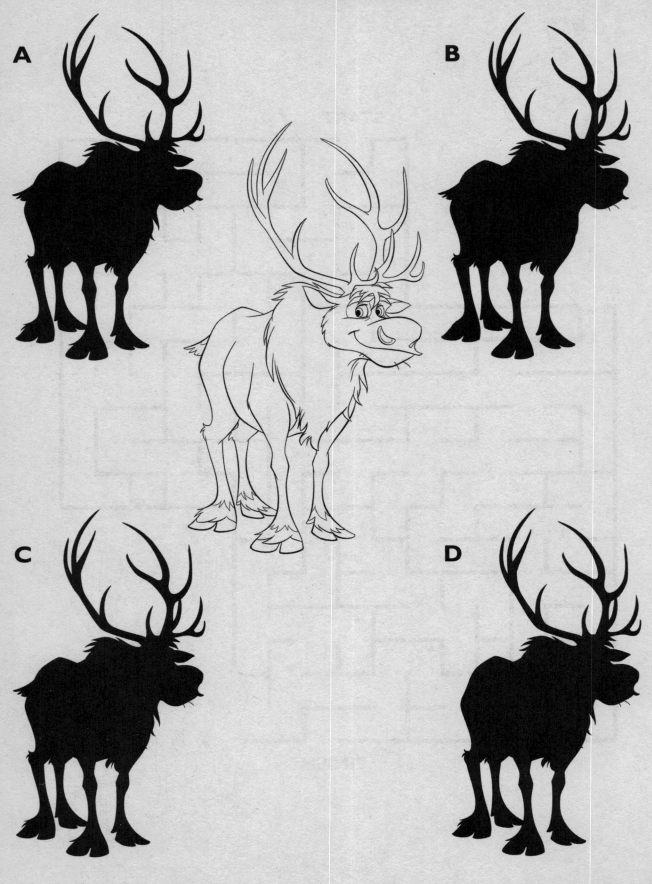

A

B

C

D

Use the grid to draw a picture of Sven.

How many times can you find **COLD** in the puzzle?
Look up, down, forward, and backward.

C	O	L	D	D
O	C	O	L	D
C	O	L	D	L
L	L	D	L	O
L	D	L	O	C

Draw new antlers on Sven.

Sven's favorite snack is carrots.
Solve the maze to help Sven get
to the carrots.

START

FINISH

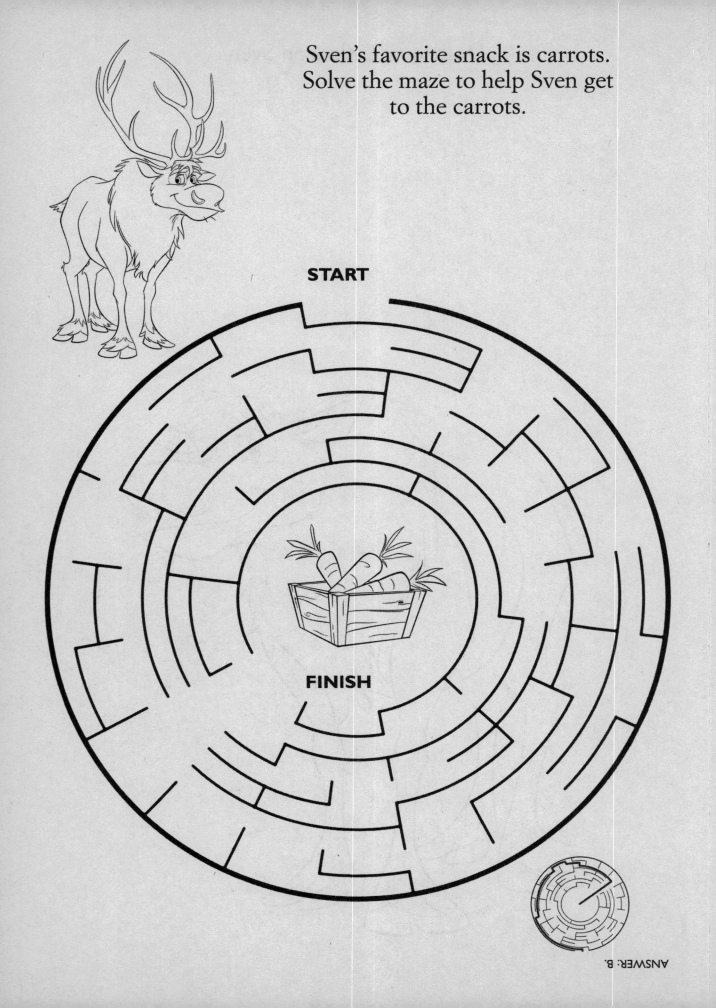

Draw a big carrot for Sven to eat!

Solve the maze to help Sven find Kristoff.

START

FINISH

ANSWER:

Draw a line from each character to its shadow.

I

A

2

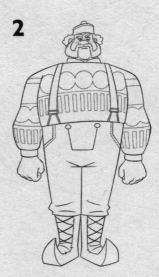

B

3

C

1-B; 2-C; 3-A.

Kristoff agrees to help Anna search for her sister.

Anna and Kristoff are chased by wolves!

How many times can you find **SLED** in the puzzle?
Look up, down, forward, and backward.

S	S	L	E	D	D
L	L	S	L	E	D
E	E	D	E	L	S
D	D	E	L	S	D

The wolf chase ends with a terrible crash!
Anna and Sven pull Kristoff to safety.

Kristoff's sled is destroyed!
But Anna still needs his help to find her sister.

What is the name of this snowman? Use the key to find out.

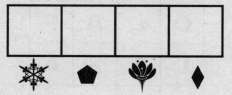

ANSWER: Olaf.

How many times can you find **OLAF** in the puzzle?
Look up, down, forward, and backward.

L	O	F	O
O	L	A	F
L	A	F	A
A	F	F	L
F	A	L	O

Circle the picture of Olaf that is different.

Draw another arm for Olaf.

Anna, Kristoff, and Sven meet Olaf in Elsa's icy wonderland.

How many words can you make using the letters in
WONDERLAND?

Draw your own snowman like Olaf.

Color Sven and Olaf.

Color Kristoff.

Circle Olaf's shadow.

A

B

C

D

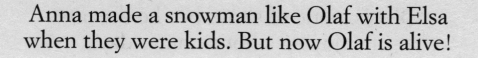

Anna made a snowman like Olaf with Elsa
when they were kids. But now Olaf is alive!

Olaf is made of snow, but he dreams
of enjoying a hot summer day!

How many times can you find **SNOW** in the puzzle?
Look up, down, forward, and backward.

W	O	N	S	O	W
S	N	O	W	O	O
S	W	O	N	S	N
S	N	W	O	N	S

Olaf thinks Sven wants to give him a kiss!

What does Sven want to do? To find out, start at the arrow and, going clockwise around the circle, write every other letter in order on the blanks.

_ _ _ _ _ _ _ _ _ _ _ _

_ _ _ _ _ _ _ _ ,

_ _ _ _ _ _ _ _ _ _ _ _ !

© Disney

Circle snowflakes that have the letters in Olaf's name.

How many times can you find **SVEN** in the puzzle?
Look up, down, forward, and backward.

N	N	S	V	E	N
N	E	V	S	S	E
S	V	E	N	S	V
V	S	N	E	V	S
E	N	N	E	V	S
N	S	V	E	N	N

Draw a new nose for Olaf.

Look up, down, forward, and backward to find the names below.

Anna Elsa Kristoff Sven Olaf

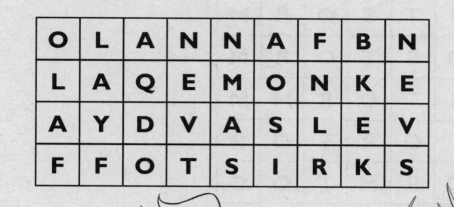

O	L	A	N	N	A	F	B	N
L	A	Q	E	M	O	N	K	E
A	Y	D	V	A	S	L	E	V
F	F	O	T	S	I	R	K	S

How many times can you find **STORM** in the puzzle?
Look up, down, forward, and backward.

S	T	S	O	R	M
O	S	T	O	R	M
S	T	O	R	M	M
T	O	R	T	O	R
O	R	M	T	O	O
R	M	O	T	S	T
M	M	R	O	T	S

Anna is ready to climb a wall of ice to
find Elsa, but Olaf has a better idea!

Solve the maze to help Anna and
her friends reach Elsa's ice palace.

FINISH

START

How many times can you find **PALACE** in the puzzle?
Look up, down, forward, backward, and diagonally.

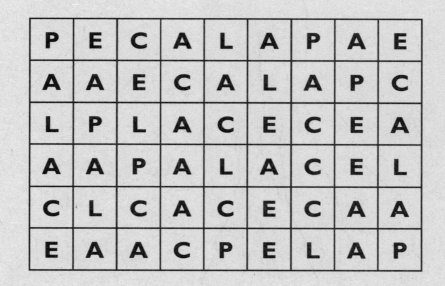

P	E	C	A	L	A	P	A	E
A	A	E	C	A	L	A	P	C
L	P	L	A	C	E	C	E	A
A	A	P	A	L	A	C	E	L
C	L	C	A	C	E	C	A	A
E	A	A	C	P	E	L	A	P

© Disney

ANSWER: 6.

Elsa's ice palace is beautiful!

Draw your own ice palace on this page.

Elsa is impressed that Anna made it all the way to her ice palace.

Color the Snow Queen.

Anna begs Elsa to return home. She misses her sister!
But Elsa wants to stay in her ice palace.

Elsa doesn't want to go home, but she is the only one who can stop the winter storm and save Arendelle!

How many times can you find **ANNA** in the puzzle?
Look up, down, forward, and backward.

A	A	N	A	A	N
N	N	A	N	N	A
N	N	N	N	N	N
A	N	N	A	A	N
A	N	A	N	N	A

Elsa accidentally hits Anna with an icy blast!

Elsa is afraid of hurting people.
She refuses to go home with Anna.

To find out the name of this giant snowman, circle every third letter. Then write those letters in order on the blanks.

ZAMBGAXYRNQSZAHRT MBGAXYLRNLQRONMW

— — — — — — — — — — — — —

How many words can you make using the letters in **MARSHMALLOW**?

_____   _____

_____   _____

_____   _____

_____   _____

_____   _____

_____   _____

_____   _____

_____   _____

Elsa creates Marshmallow to scare Anna
and her friends off the mountain.

Draw your own snow monster.

Draw a carrot nose on Marshmallow
to make him look like Olaf!

What would you make if you had ice powers? Draw it.

Marshmallow is looking for Anna and Kristoff!
Solve the maze to help them find Olaf and escape.

START

FINISH

ANSWER:

Marshmallow chases Anna and Kristoff to the mountain's edge.

Anna and Kristoff rappel down the mountain.

How many words can you make using the letters in
SNOWMAN?

_____ _____

_____ _____

_____ _____

_____ _____

_____ _____

_____ _____

_____ _____

POSSIBLE ANSWERS: Am, an, as, ma, man, mow, no, now, on, one, own, saw, snow, so, son, swam, swan, was, woman, and won.

Solve the maze to help Sven find Olaf!

START

FINISH

ANSWER:

Draw a mountain for Anna and Kristoff to climb.

Oh, no! Anna's hair is turning white because of Elsa's icy blast!

Counting Kristoff! How many are there?

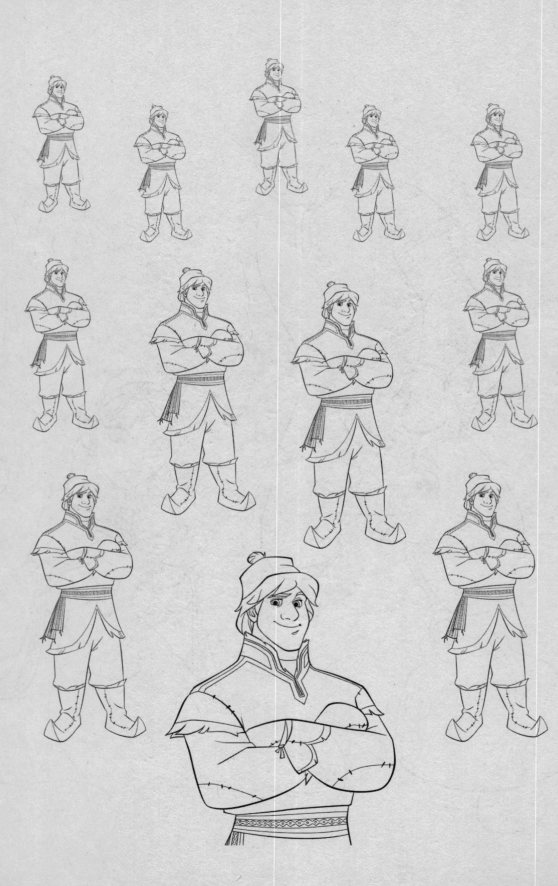

How many times can you find **ICE** in the puzzle?
Look up, down, forward, backward, and diagonally.

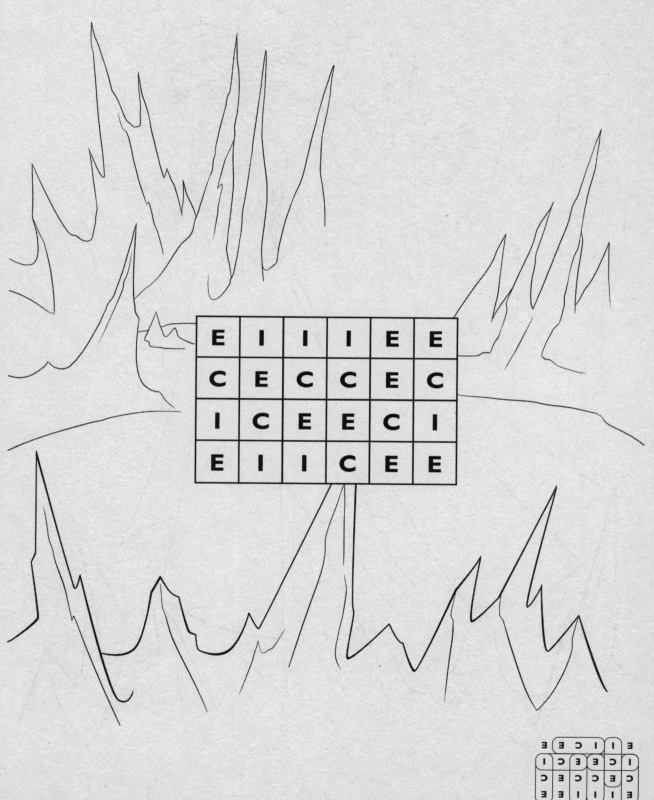

E	I	I	I	E	E
C	E	C	C	E	C
I	C	E	E	C	I
E	I	I	C	E	E

Elsa worries about how she will stop
the winter storm and save Arendelle.

Design a new dress for Elsa, the Snow Queen.

Anna's horse returns to Arendelle without her.

Hans heads off to find Anna.

Solve the maze to help Hans reach the North Mountain.

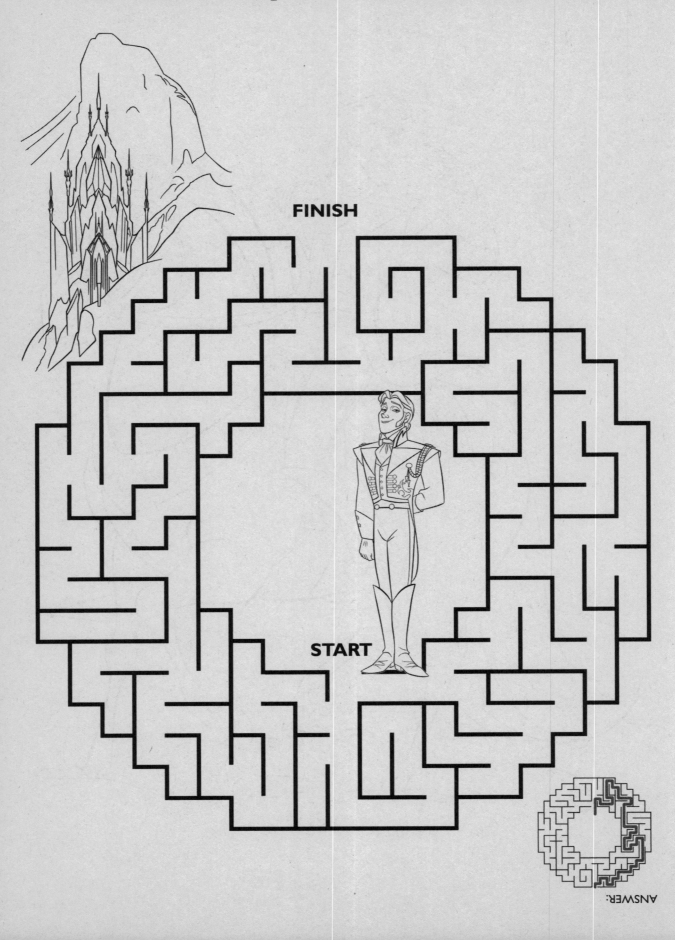

FINISH

START

ANSWER:

Decorate the horse that Hans is riding.

Draw a horse on this page.

Solve the maze to help Olaf, Kristoff, and Anna find the trolls.

START

FINISH

ANSWER:

Anna learns that her heart is turning to ice!
Use the key to find out what can save her.

Kristoff thinks the magical trolls can help Anna.

Draw your own troll on this page.

Count the trolls on this page. How many are there?

How many times can you find **TROLL** in the puzzle?
Look up, down, forward, and backward.

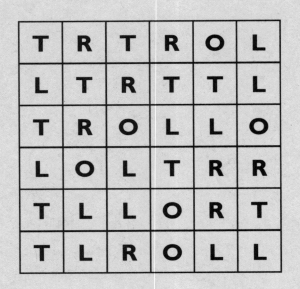

T	R	T	R	O	L
L	T	R	T	T	L
T	R	O	L	L	O
L	O	L	T	R	R
T	L	L	O	R	T
T	L	R	O	L	L

Anna meets a very old troll.

The old troll is very worried. Only an act of
true love can save Anna from becoming frozen.

Use the grid to draw a picture of the troll.

Draw a new hat for Kristoff.

Draw something you like to do in the snow!

Anna starts to freeze! Solve the maze
to help Kristoff get her back to Arendelle.

START

FINISH

Kristoff hopes that a kiss from Hans,
Anna's true love, will save her.

Marshmallow battles the royal guards who have
arrived at Elsa's palace with Hans.

Help Hans reach Elsa.

START

FINISH

ANSWER: C.

One of the guards corners Elsa!

Elsa defends herself with icy spikes!
Hans tells her to stop.

To find out what Hans wants to do, start at the arrow and, going clockwise around the circle, write the letters in order on the blanks.

_ _ _ _   _ _ _ _

_ _   _ _ _ _   _ _ _ _   _ _ _ _

_ _ _ _ _   _ _ _ _ .

Elsa won't leave her ice palace without a fight!

An arrow from one of the duke's guards hits a chandelier!
Elsa races out of harm's way in the nick of time!

The Snow Queen has been captured!
Solve the maze to return her to Arendelle.

START

FINISH

ANSWER:

Hans locks Elsa in a dungeon to protect the kingdom.

Kristoff arrives at the castle with Anna.
She is quickly rushed off before they can say goodbye.

Anna needs a kiss from her true love to save her.
But Hans won't kiss her!

Hans reveals his evil plan to take over the kingdom. He puts out the fire that has been keeping Anna warm. Now she will freeze!

So many Svens! How many are there?

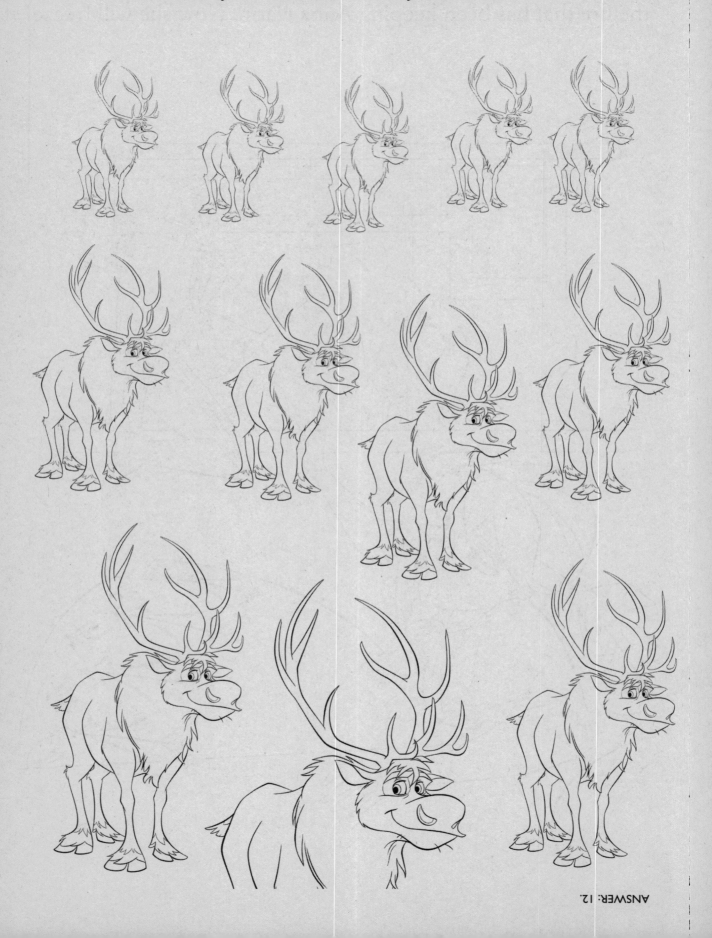

How many times can you find HANS in the puzzle?
Look up, down, forward, and backward.

S	N	A	H
N	H	S	A
H	A	N	S
H	N	A	A
N	S	H	H

ANSWER: 4.

Anna doesn't have the strength to warn
her sister about Hans. She's so very cold!

Hans spreads lies so he can take over the throne.
He tells everyone that Queen Elsa has killed Anna!

Elsa blasts out of the dungeon!

Sven wants Kristoff to return to Arendelle to be with Anna.

What is Kristoff saying? Write it in the speech balloon.

Solve the maze to help Olaf find Anna!

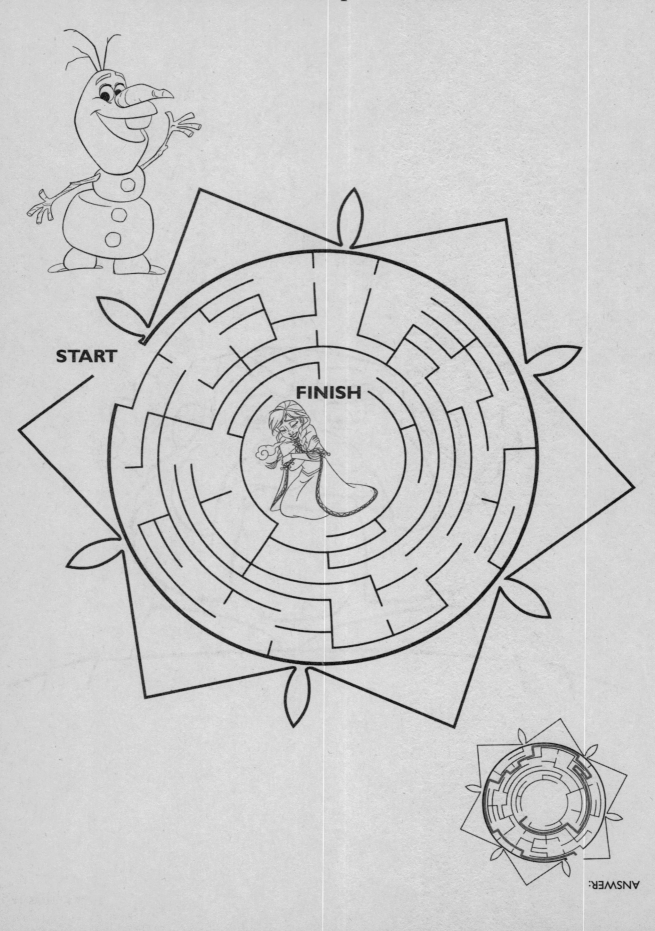

START

FINISH

Olaf discovers that Kristoff loves Anna!
Only a kiss from Kristoff can save her.

Kissing Kristoff is Anna's only hope. Olaf helps Anna escape!

Anna has very little time left. She is turning to ice!

Elsa thinks her sister is gone! She blames herself.

Anna runs to Kristoff.

Hans sneaks up on Elsa.

Hans is going to hurt Elsa!
Anna saves her sister just as she freezes solid.

Cross out all the pictures of Hans.
How many pictures of Kristoff are left?

Draw a line from each picture to its close-up.

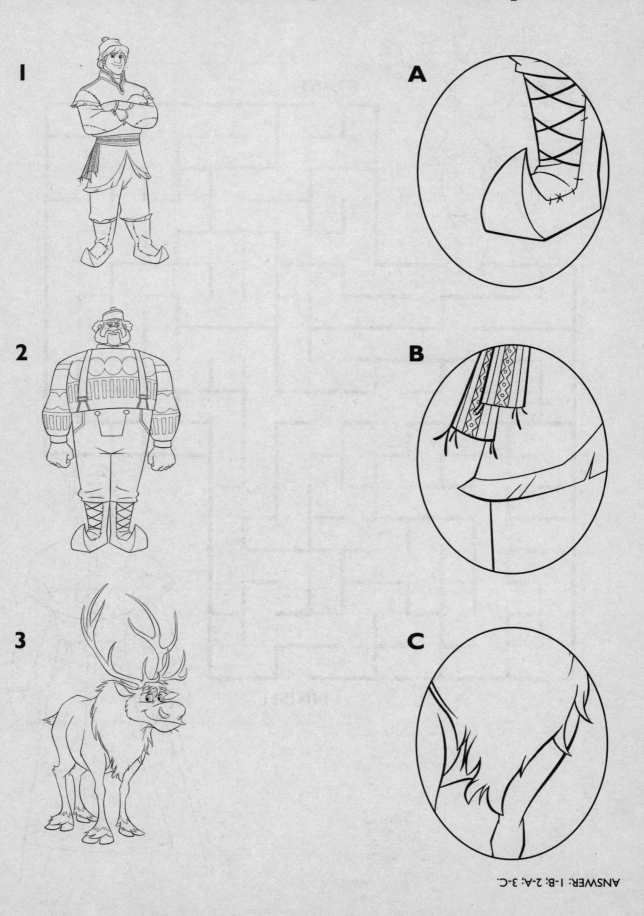

1

2

3

A

B

C

ANSWER: 1-B; 2-A; 3-C.

Solve the maze to help Kristoff stop Hans.

START

FINISH

Kristoff races to the rescue!

Kristoff battles Hans! With a friend, take turns connecting two dots with a straight line. If the line you draw completes a box, put your initials in it and take another turn. Count one point for squares containing your initials. When all the dots have been connected, the player with more points wins!

Play again! With a friend, take turns connecting two dots with a straight line. If the line you draw completes a box, put your initials in it and take another turn. Count one point for squares containing your initials. When all the dots have been connected, the player with more points wins!

Elsa can't believe her sister is frozen!
Suddenly, Anna starts to thaw!

How many times can you find **FROZEN** in the puzzle?
Look up, down, forward, and backward.

N	F	F	R	O	Z	E	N
E	E	F	R	O	Z	E	N	E
F	R	O	Z	E	N	O	Z
F	O	R	Z	Z	R	F	O
Z	Z	F	R	Z	E	N	R
F	E	N	E	Z	O	R	F
N	N	E	Z	O	R	F	N

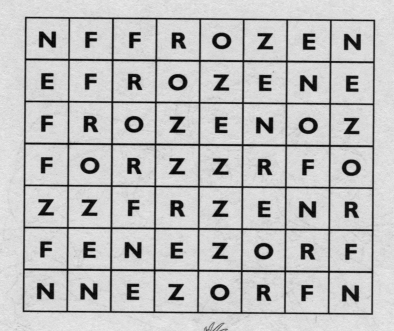

Anna's frozen heart began to melt when she saved her sister.
It was an act of true love!

Anna has taught Elsa about love and not being afraid.
Elsa uses her magic to bring back summer!

Help Elsa find Olaf.

START

FINISH

With a little magic from Elsa, Olaf can enjoy the warm weather!

To find out what Olaf likes, start at the arrow and, going clockwise around the circle, write the letters in order on the blanks.

_ _ _ _ _ _ _ _ _ _

_ _ _ _ _ _ _ _ _

_ _ _ _ _ _ _ _ _ !

Anna won't be tricked by Hans anymore!

Anna vs. Hans! With a friend, take turns connecting two dots with a straight line. If the line you draw completes a box, put your initials in it and take another turn. Count one point for squares containing your initials. When all the dots have been connected, the player with more points wins!

Play again! With a friend, take turns
connecting two dots with a straight line.
If the line you draw completes a box,
put your initials in it and take another
turn. Count one point for squares
containing your initials. When all the
dots have been connected, the player
with more points wins!

Everyone is glad that summer has returned
to Arendelle—especially Olaf!

How many times can you find **SUMMER** in the puzzle?
Look up, down, forward, and backward.

R	S	U	M	M	E	R	M
E	U	S	U	M	M	E	R
M	M	S	R	R	S	M	R
M	M	E	S	S	R	M	R
U	E	R	E	M	M	U	S
S	R	U	M	M	E	S	R

© Disney

Anna thanks Kristoff for helping to save her sister.

Who is Anna's true love? To find out,
close one eye and slowly tilt the page away from you.

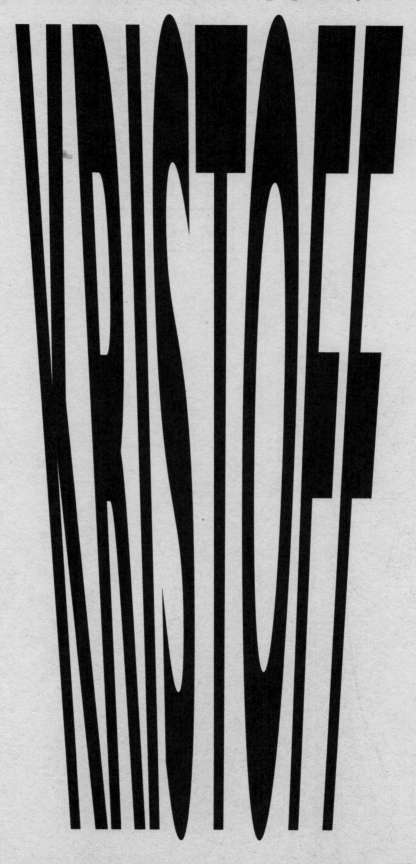

How many times can you find **LOVE** in the puzzle?
Look up, down, forward, backward, and diagonally.

L	O	L	E	E
O	L	O	V	E
L	O	V	E	V
L	V	E	L	O
V	E	V	O	L

Draw of a picture of someone you love!

Draw a new outfit for Kristoff.

Anna thanks Sven for his help, too!

Finally, Anna and Elsa can play together again!
Elsa makes another winter wonderland in the Great Hall.

Anna and Elsa fix their favorite snowman!

How many words can you make using the letters in
SNOWFLAKE?

_____   _____

_____   _____

_____   _____

_____   _____

_____   _____

_____   _____

_____   _____

_____   _____

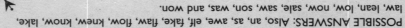

Count the snowflakes on this page. How many are there?

Find the matching snowflakes.

Anna and Elsa are friends again.
Nothing will keep these sisters apart!

What are they saying? Write it in their speech balloons.